Paws for a Cause

Read all the Diary of a Pug books!

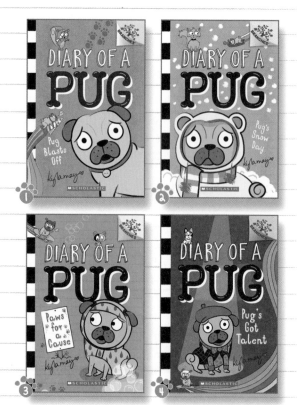

DIARY OF A PUG — Pug Blasts Off — kyla may — SCHOLASTIC — 1

DIARY OF A PUG — Pug's Snow Day — kyla may — SCHOLASTIC — 2

DIARY OF A PUG — Paws for a Cause — kyla may — SCHOLASTIC — 3

DIARY OF A PUG — Pug's Got Talent — kyla may — SCHOLASTIC — 4

More books coming soon!

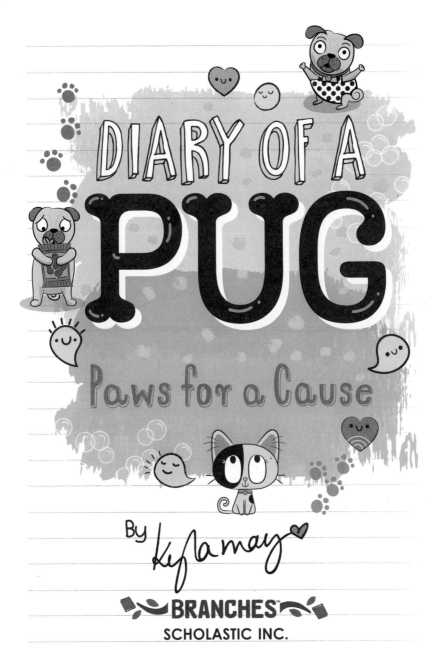

DIARY OF A PUG

Paws for a Cause

By Kyla May

BRANCHES

SCHOLASTIC INC.

To my loving dad and sister

Special thanks to Sonia Sander

Art copyright © 2020 by Kyla May Dinsmore
Text copyright © 2020 by Scholastic Inc.

Library of Congress Control Number: 2020930346
ISBN 978-1-338-53010-0 (hardcover) / ISBN 978-1-338-53009-4 (paperback)

10 9 8 7 6 5 4 3 2 1   20 21 22 23 24

Printed in China   62
First edition, July 2020
Edited by Katie Woehr
Book design by Kyla May and Sarah Dvojack

Table of Contents

1. Paws Made for Walking........1

2. Paws for a Kiss........................11

3. Playful Paws...............................21

4. Paws for a Cause..................28

5. Pool Paw-ty................................38

6. Muddy Paws.............................45

7. Posh Paws................................58

8. A Round of Ap-paws............66

Chapter 1

PAWS MADE FOR WALKING

MONDAY

Dear Diary,

BARON VON BUBBLES here. But everyone calls me BUB.

Things have been pretty quiet lately. Today was another story! But first, here are some things to know about me:

I always dress to impress. (Some people say I'm the cutest pug on the planet.)

I make many different faces:

Snuggling Bella Face

Begging for a Treat Face

Nervous Face (also known as the I Just Farted Face)

Face for Duchess

Move it, Bubby-kins, or I'll move you.

DUCHESS

(Duchess thinks she's the boss.)

Face for Nutz

What are you up to NOW?

Nothing. Nothing at all!

NUTZ

(Nutz is always stealing something.)

Here are some of my favorite things:

BEAR

PEANUT BUTTER
TREATS

MY BEST FRIEND LUNA
(Even if she
does love
water!)

That's right! Water is still NOT my favorite!

Bella laughed so hard the first time I jumped into a bubble bath. I had no idea there was WATER under the bubbles! (That's how I got my name, by the way.)

BELLA

Eeeekkk!

Now I'm okay with baths, rain, and snow when I have to be. But wet kisses! YUCK! No one is allowed to give me one of those.

Well, except for Bella. She adopted me from a pet adoption fair when I was just a pup.

I love giving you kisses!

Diary, you won't believe what Bella and I found on our walk today. It was a lost kitten!

Poor baby. She is so cold, she is shaking.

Who left you here all alone?

Meeoooowww!

Meeoooowww!

Bella scooped up the kitten, and we took her home.

Back in our kitchen, we fed the kitten.

Here, you can use my bowl.

WATER

9

Diary, I had the hardest time falling asleep. I know I'm Bella's favorite. But what if Bella keeps this kitten and forgets about ME?

❋ x Chapter 2 ❋ x

PAWS FOR A KISS

TUESDAY

Dear Diary,

This morning I woke up and found the kitten curled up next to me. At first I was annoyed. Then she gave me a kiss on my nose and my heart melted.

Meow.

I guess kisses from you are okay, too.

While we waited for Bella to wake up,
I lent the kitty one of my toys.

You won't believe this, Diary! When Bella woke up, she said hello to the kitten first!

Of course, Duchess tried to make me feel worse.

After breakfast, Bella's mom said we had to take the kitten to the animal shelter first-thing tomorrow morning. She said they will find a great home for her.

Bella was heartbroken. I was sad, too, but mostly I was glad I would have Bella to myself again.

Mom, can't we please keep her?

I'm sorry, Bella. Two pets is my limit.

The kitten seemed sad. So I tried to cheer her up.

You will have fun at the shelter while you wait for your new family.

I could tell Bella was really sad and wanted to stay in her room. But we had plans with our best friends, Jack and Luna.

Okay, okay. Let's go next door.

Jack and Luna were waiting for us. Luna loved the kitten. She gave her a big slobbery kiss.

I'm not a fan of Luna's kisses either, Kitty. But it's a small price to pay to be her BFF.

Bella told Jack that we had to take the kitten to the animal shelter tomorrow.

We adopted Luna from that shelter. If you want, we can go with you.

Great!

We spent the rest of the day playing in the yard. The kitten followed my every step.

Oh Bubby, how cute. She is copying you.

Sorry, Kitty. You'll never be THIS cute!

Tonight, we all went to bed feeling sad.

It's going to be hard to say good-bye.

You can say that again.

Chapter 3

PLAYFUL PAWS

WEDNESDAY

Dear Diary,

The shelter was not like I thought it would be. The workers were nice, but it was loud and crowded and it smelled funny.

I don't think Kitty likes it here.

You're okay, Kitty. It's different here, isn't it?

The kitten was afraid. Luckily, the workers let Bella hold her while we walked around. Bella and Jack asked tons of questions.

Where will she sleep? Will she be with other kittens?

Do you check on the animals at night? How long do pets wait to get a home?

They showed us the play area for the kittens last. It was pretty sad looking. There were no toys.

How come they don't have toys to play with?

We can't afford toys. All our money comes from donations. We use the donations to pay for food and medicine. There isn't money left over for toys.

Diary, can you believe the kittens don't have toys to play with? I decided right then to leave my toy with the kitten.

We said good-bye to the kitten and left the shelter. But we were sad on the way home.

I wish we could help the shelter.

What can we do? We don't have any money.

When we were almost home, Luna spotted a sprinkler. You know there is no stopping Luna when she sees water.

The day didn't end well. Thanks to Luna we were all covered in mud. Bella had to give me a bath.

I usually pay the pet groomer to wash Bub, but you did a great job, Bella!

Bubby, are you thinking what I'm thinking?

That I really DON'T like baths?

Come on. Let's get you dried off. Mom just gave me an idea about how we can help the shelter. Tomorrow is going to be a busy day!

Chapter 4

PAWS FOR A CAUSE

THURSDAY

Dear Diary,

It is never good news for me when Bella wakes me up early. It usually means work, work, and more work.

Come on, sleepyhead. We need to go tell Jack and Luna about my plan.

Plan? At this hour?

It was so early, we had to sit outside
and wait for our BFFs to wake up.

Here they come, Bub.
I told you Jack and
Luna get up early.

JACK &
LUNA'S
BACK
DOOR

Not as early
as we got up.

Oh, Diary, Jack and Luna are HUGE fans of Bella's idea. But I am not. Guess what she wants to do? She wants to run a pet wash. That means lots of WATER!

We can run a pet wash on Saturday to raise money for toys for the shelter!

Great idea!

I'M IN!

Maybe later. I'm going back to bed.

Bella stopped me before I got too far. She needed me to help her drag out supplies for the pet wash.

Jack brought over Luna's pool. Luna was so excited. She couldn't stop running in circles.

I can't wait! I can't wait!

Easy, girl. You're going to pop the pool.

When we had all the supplies together, Jack pulled a tarp over the pile.

We can set up tomorrow. Did we forget anything?

We'll need treats to reward the pets after their baths.

I can be in charge of treats!

I was sure we were done for the day.
But Bella said we had one more thing to do.

We have to make a sign for our pet wash so people will come!

The sign needs a catchy line so people will stop and read it!

I know. "Look out! SPLASH ZONE!"

I was a big help with the sign.

We put the sign in front of the house.

Chapter 5

POOL PAW-TY

FRIDAY

Dear Diary,

Did you know "trial run" means "practice run"? Bella and Jack wanted to give Luna and me baths to practice for the pet wash! Since Luna loves water, she was happy to help. But you know I was NOT.

Who is ready for a bath?

Me!

Maybe Luna's trial run will go so well, they won't need me.

Diary, Luna's trial did not go well. Luna went wild!

Luna, they are supposed to wash YOU. You are not supposed to wash everyone else.

There was water everywhere! I could tell Bella and Jack were worried their pet-wash plan might not work. I was hoping they might give up. But no such luck.

Let's try washing Bub.

Since I do NOT like water, I quietly sat there and waited for it to be over.

This is a piece of cake.

We can totally run a pet wash!

This is all for you, Kitty.

I hope the pets tomorrow are like me and not like Luna. Or this pet wash is going to be a total disaster.

My plan tomorrow is to stay dry at all costs. Hmm. Is that Nutz snooping around over there?

If tomorrow is anything like today, my plan will be easy to pull off.

It had been a very long day, Diary. The last thing I needed was nosy Nutz.

What are you doing here, Nuthead?

Don't be like that. I'm just seeing what the waterworks are about.

Great. Now I have to watch out for water AND Nutz tomorrow.

Chapter 6

MUDDY PAWS

SATURDAY

Dear Diary,

Today was Pet Wash Day. I had the perfect outfit.

Oh Bubby, you are going to melt.

But I'll be dry!

Diary, the pet wash did NOT go as planned. Our first customer brought a litter of puppies! She paid us and left for an hour.

We never practiced with more than one pet!

Look—they are asleep. Just don't wake them up.

Too late.

Of course the puppies woke up. When we started their bath, they would not stay in the pool.

Back in the bath, pup.

This way, champ.

We were so focused on the puppies, we forgot to turn the hose off. Bubbles flowed all over the lawn.

I ran to the hose and pinched it closed
so the water would stop.

While we were busy, Nutz swung down from his tree.

I could see where Nutz was headed—the peanut butter treats! I could not let him steal them. But if I let go of the hose, I would get wet. It was a hard choice.

I decided to save the treats. I let go of the hose and called for help with Nutz.

HELP, Luna!

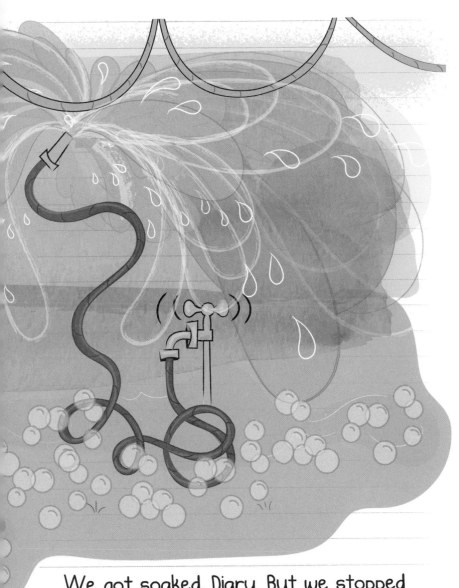

We got soaked, Diary. But we stopped
Nutz from getting the treats.

Jack turned off the hose. We gathered the puppies. But the yard was a muddy mess. There was no way we could wash more pets today.

Bella took down our sign.

We won't be able to help the shelter, Bubby.

I had not thought of that, Diary. I got my treats, but no pet wash meant no treats for the kitten.

I'm sorry.

Paws for a Cause
Pet Wash this Saturday!

When the owner came back to get her puppies, she was not happy. I didn't blame her. Bella gave her back her money.

I'm glad I drove my truck over. There's no way I'd put these pups in my car, since I just took it through the car wash.

Diary, something the owner said cheered Bella up! Bella begged the owner to bring the puppies back for another wash.

You gave me an idea. Give us a second chance tomorrow? To help the shelter?

I guess you can't make my pups dirtier than they are now. I'll think about it.

Maybe we can help Kitty after all!

Chapter 7

POSH PAWS

SUNDAY

Dear Diary,

Bella woke us up bright and early AGAIN.

Come on, slowpoke! I know how we can fix our pet wash.

Jack and Luna met us outside. There was a big pile of supplies. Bella had been up for hours!

It took a few hours, but we built our pet wash.

GETTING THERE...

...DONE!

Let's turn on the hose and see if it works.

Luna will love to try it out.

Luna headed inside the pet washer. Jack sprayed her with soap. The pet washer scrubbed and rinsed.

Bella worked the hair dryers. I took charge of the treats. (Someone had to keep them from Nutz.)

You're almost dry, Luna.

Come and get your treat!

Paws for a Cause

~~Pet Wash this Saturday!~~ TODAY!

The pet wash was back on! Jack fixed our sign and put it back up.

Guess what, Diary? The puppies came back! Other pets from the neighborhood came, too.

Hold on tight. Here we go!

Good job, pups!

At the end of the day, we were tired and dirty. But we had cleaned a lot of pets and raised money for the shelter.

Great job, Bub and Luna. The rest of the treats are all yours!

Yummy!

We helped Kitty AND I get treats? Yes, please!

Chapter 8

A ROUND OF AP-PAWS

MONDAY

Dear Diary,

We went back to the animal shelter today. It was my turn to get up early. I couldn't wait to see the kitten.

LICK

Get up! Get up!

We used the money we raised to buy lots of toys to donate to the shelter.

Hurry up! I can't wait to surprise the pets.

The workers at the shelter took us straight to the kitten.

We really missed you.

The workers told us the kitten was going to be adopted! A family that lives around the corner from us was taking her home.

Then we handed out the toys to the pets. They were so happy!

We spent all afternoon playing with the pets.

The workers thanked us for the toys. They even asked us to come back and play with the animals.

I never knew my little paws could make such a big difference, Diary! Who should we help next?

About the Creator

Kyla May ♥

Kyla May is an Australian illustrator, writer, and designer. In addition to books, Kyla creates animation. She lives by the beach in Victoria, Australia, with her three daughters and her daughter's pug called Bear.

HOW MUCH DO YOU KNOW ABOUT
DIARY OF A PUG
Paws for a Cause?

 When Bub and Bella drop me off at the shelter, there aren't any toys to play with. Why doesn't the shelter have any toys?

 Even though Bub and I are best friends, sometimes we like different things. What is the one thing I love but Bub hates?

 When I choose to let go of the hose, what am I trying to save? Why is it a hard decision for me to let go of the hose?

 What gives me the idea to run the pet wash like a car wash? Reread pages 56–57.

 Imagine you want to raise money for a cause you care about. What cause would you choose? How would you raise the money? Write your fundraising plan.

scholastic.com/branches